The Mouse
and the
Magic Socks

Written by
Maggie Freeman

Illustrated by
Brian Fitzgerald

"I'm lost, I'm lost," says the sad mouse in the snowy forest.

At last he comes to a door. He opens it and squeezes inside.

Wrapped up in blankets, in a nest of dry leaves, is a big bear, fast asleep under a fat duvet. He wears bright stripey socks and snores very loudly.

The bear is toasty and warm to snuggle up to, and Mouse curls up in the fur on his chest, and goes up and down with the bear's breathing.

After a while, Mouse gets hungry.

"I'm hungry," says Mouse.

He nibbles the blankets, but they taste horrid.

He tries the dry leaves, but they are sharp and nasty.

He tastes a red stripe on the bear's socks. "Yum," says Mouse. "Tasty socks."

"Grrrr," says the bear, without opening his eyes.

"Eeek," says Mouse.

Mouse runs away, pulling the red stripe after him. But it escapes and unravels like a red ribbon, twisting and turning out of the door
    down the steps
        over the snow to a cave
            with the mouse bouncing after it
                to a treasure chest of
                    red raspberries.

"YUM!" says Mouse. He sits and eats raspberries until he's full up.

Then he goes back to the bear's home and curls up in the fur on the sleeping bear's chest.

Later, Mouse gets hungry again.

"I'm ever so hungry," he says.

He bites a hole in the duvet, but its filling makes him sneeze.

He has a go at the bear's hat, but he hates it.

He tastes a blue stripe on the bear's socks.

"Yum," he says. "Yummy socks."

"Grrrrrrr," says the bear, opening one eye.

"Eeeeeek," squeaks Mouse.

Mouse runs away, pulling the blue stripe after him. But it escapes like a quick snake,
  slipping out of the door
    down the steps
      and slithering over the snow to a cave,
        with the mouse hopping after it
          to a basket heaped
            high with
              blueberries.

"YUM!" says the mouse. He eats and eats blueberries until he can't eat any more.

Then he goes back to the bear's home and curls up in the fur on the sleeping bear's chest.

Much later, Mouse gets hungrier than ever. "I'm SO, SO hungry," he says.

He hates the taste of the blankets and the duvet.

He won't touch the dry leaves or the hat.

But the gold stripe on Bear's socks is sweet when Mouse tastes it.

"It tastes best of all," he says. "YUM!"

"Grrrrrrrrrrrrrr," says Bear, opening his two eyes. "WHO'S BEEN NIBBLING HOLES IN MY SOCKS? WHO HAS PULLED THEM TO PIECES SO I'VE GOT BARE PAWS?"

"Eeeeeeeeek," squeaks Mouse.

Mouse runs away as fast as he can, with the end of the gold stripe in his mouth. Bear pounds after him.

But the stripe escapes like a gold stream, flowing down the steps
    cutting across the snow
        sparkling in the sunshine
            swishing between the trees of the forest
                with Mouse jumping after it
and Bear jumping after Mouse, till they come to a cave full of jars of golden honey.

"Oh bliss," says Bear.
"Oh yum," says Mouse.

Much, much later, Mouse and Bear are both sticky and funny and full up with honey.

Slowly they go back to the bear's home.

Bear gets under his duvet and blankets. Full of honey, he falls fast asleep.

Mouse curls up in the fur on Bear's chest, and falls fast asleep too.

Both Bear and Mouse are dreaming happily of honey.